This book
belongs to

....

Cuddle's Fan Pages

Here's what other children have to say about their favourite kitten and her latest adventure!

"I liked the story about sleepovers because I have never been to one. I also liked when they played princesses, because I have always wanted to be a princess." Kittie, age 7

"My favourite bit of the story was when they met a princess called Victoria in a tree and they thought she was a thief. It was funny. I think there should be more stories about Cuddle." Emily, age 8

"I liked the bit when Olivia was so excited about her first sleepover. I loved it when Cuddle appeared. I also liked the part when they dressed up in Victoria's room."
Sophia, age 6

"I didn't just like a little bit - I liked ALL of it!" Bethany, age 6

"I really liked this Cuddle story because it's about a sleepover and I would love to have a sleepover with my best friend too. The girls were very lucky to meet a real princess. I liked it when they all went to the ball together."
Maia, age 6

"This was the best Cuddle book ever! I really liked the princess who was a tomboy and didn't want to wear a frilly dress. The king and queen were happy when she went to the ball and I liked that." Ava, age 8

"I liked it when they went to the ball, and also the end bit when they were home in bed because they get to sleep! I loved the story, it was just right for me." Lucina, age 6

Princess Party Sleepover

Other books about
Cuddle the Cutest Kitten:

Magical Friends
Superstar Dreams
School of Spells

Cuddle

★ the cutest kitten ★

Princess Party Sleepover

by Hayley Daze
illustrated by Ann Kronheimer
cover illustrated by Amanda Gulliver

A catalogue record for this book is available from the British Library

Published by Ladybird Books Ltd
A Penguin Company
Penguin Books Ltd., 80 Strand, London WC2R 0RL, UK
Penguin Books Australia Ltd., Camberwell, Victoria, Australia
Penguin Group (NZ) 67 Apollo Drive, Rosedale,
North Shore 0632, New Zealand

001 – 1 3 5 7 9 10 8 6 4 2
Series created by Working Partners Limited, London WC1X 9HH
Text © Working Partners Ltd MMXI
Cover illustration © Working Partners Ltd MMXI
Interior illustrations © Ladybird Books Ltd MMXI

Special thanks to Elizabeth Galloway

ISBN: 978-1-40930-852-2
Printed in England

To Daisy and Elizabeth

Cuddle the kitten has black-and-white fur,
A cute crooked tail, and a very loud purr.
Her two best friends, Olivia and Grace,
Know Cuddle's world is a special place!

Just give her a cuddle, then everything spins;
A twitch of her whiskers, and magic begins!
So if you see a sunbeam, and hear Cuddle's bell,
You can join in the adventures as well!

Contents

Chapter One
Sunset Surprise

It was a warm summer's evening and Olivia's bedroom window was wide open. Purple wisteria flowers nodded against the sill and furry bumblebees buzzed round them, collecting the last of the day's pollen. The setting sun made the houses of Catterton glow a rosy pink.

"Our first sleepover!" Olivia

squealed, twirling in her pink,
ruffled nightie.

"I've never been to a sleepover
before," Grace said, doing up the last
button of her favourite star-patterned
pyjamas. "What should we do first?"

The girls flopped on Olivia's bed,
which had a fluffy pink duvet.

"Let's play princesses,"

Olivia suggested. She leapt to her feet, wobbling on her bed.

She wrapped her duvet round her shoulders like a royal robe.

"Ta-dah!" she said and pretended to wave at her loyal subjects.

"Hello, Your Royal Highness!" Grace said, and bowed to Olivia.

"Now it's your turn," Olivia said, jumping down to sit beside Grace. "You'd

make a lovely princess."

Grace shook her head, making her blonde hair fly about. "No way! Who wants to be a princess and have to wear dresses and go to boring parties? Yuck!"

Olivia stared open-mouthed at her friend. "I would love to be a princess, trying on all those lovely outfits and tiaras."

Suddenly, the setting sun sent a golden beam of light directly through the open window.

"Maybe Cuddle's coming!" Olivia said, looking down into her back garden. The girls couldn't wait to see the cute magical kitten again. Cuddle always arrived in a sudden burst of sunshine and took them on amazing adventures.

Just then, a sound drifted through the window.

Jingle jangle jingle.

"That's her bell!" Grace cried.

The wisteria branch beneath Olivia's window was shaking, its flowers bobbing up and down. A tiny

white tail with a kink in its black tip
flicked out from the quivering leaves.
"Cuddle!" both girls shouted.

The kitten's green eyes flashed as
she scrambled on to the windowsill,
the silver bell on her pink collar
jangling.

She sprang between the girls into Olivia's room, landing in the middle of the bed.

"Miaow!"

Cuddle pawed Olivia's arm. Olivia scooped the kitten up, cradling her upside down to show her tummy.

"Cuddle's purring," Olivia said, her eyes shining. "That means we're going on another adventure!"

"Where are you going to take us, Cuddle?" Grace asked, nuzzling Cuddle nose to nose.

Cuddle's purr grew louder and louder, buzzing like the bumblebees outside. The girls' skin tingled all over, making them giggle.

Grace and Olivia squeezed their eyes tightly shut.

"Here we go!" Olivia said.

Chapter Two
Treetop Trouble

The girls' eyes fluttered open. They were still wearing their bedtime clothes and slippers. The evening sky was purple and stars twinkled overhead. A gravel drive stretched before them, edged on either side by flower beds. The drive ended in a bridge, stretching over what looked like a stream.

"It's a moat!" Grace said, pointing at the sparkling water. "I've heard of those. They were built around old buildings to protect them from enemies."

On the other side of the bridge was a grand house, its hundreds of windows glittering with a golden light.

Music and laughter drifted through an open doorway. On the roof fluttered a red flag with a crown on it, and the number 1853 in swirly lettering beneath it.

"It's a palace," Olivia said, clapping her hands. "And that number on the flag must be the year! Maybe a real princess lives here!"

Cuddle darted up the drive, pausing to look back at the girls.

"Miaow!" she called.

"Okay, Cuddle, we're coming," Grace said, grabbing Olivia's hand.

The girls followed Cuddle across the bridge and towards the palace. Olivia peeked through one of the open windows. Inside was a magnificent ballroom. Glittering chandeliers hung over a dancing crowd, who were swaying in time to a four-piece band. Their costumes made a swirling sea of colour. The dancers all wore masks on their faces: some decorated with feathers, others shining with jewels.

"It's a masked ball," Olivia whispered as she picked up Cuddle and twirled round to the music.

"I'd much rather climb this," Grace said, walking to a nearby tree that was almost as tall as the palace.

Cuddle sprang from Olivia's arms and scampered up the tree. "Miaow!" Cuddle said when she reached the lowest branch.

The top of the tree began to sway. Grace peered up through the branches. She thought she saw something. A bird, maybe? Handfuls of leaves rained down on Grace and Cuddle. *A big bird*, Grace thought.

"Pssst, Olivia." Grace waved at her friend.

Olivia danced over to the tree.

"What's the matter?" she asked.

"I think someone's in the tree," Grace whispered.

Olivia looked up and spotted Cuddle sitting on the lowest branch.

31

"You mean someone other than Cuddle?"

Grace nodded.

The treetop jiggled and wiggled.

Olivia clutched Grace's arm.

"Maybe it's a thief trying to steal the crown jewels!"

Grace called Cuddle as quietly as she could.

"Please come here, Cuddle."

The kitten only blinked her bright green eyes and climbed further up the tree.

"Cuddle, come back," Olivia called.

The tree's leaves shuddered and shook. "Maybe the tree is haunted," Grace said.

Then suddenly a figure burst between the branches high above.

It was heading straight for Cuddle!

Chapter Three
Princess Problems

The strange creature in the tree came to rest on Cuddle's branch. It wasn't a thief or a ghost. It was a girl about the same age as Grace and Olivia. Her hair was in two bunches. Her canvas trousers were ripped, her face was smudged with dirt and she wasn't wearing any shoes.

"Hello!" the girl called.

"How did you get up that tree?"
Grace asked.

"I climbed down from my bedroom
window," the girl said with a smile.
"I do it all the time."

"But why?" Olivia asked.

"I have to hide," the girl said. Her
eyes widened as she glanced over the

top of their heads. "From her!" She pointed behind Grace and Olivia and ducked out of sight.

A girl in a plain grey dress and a white apron marched straight over to the tree. The girl was a little older than Grace and Olivia, with brown hair woven into a French plait.

"I know you're up there!" the girl shouted. "You need to climb down."

"Do you promise I won't have to go to the ball?" the girl in the tree called back.

"You *must* go to the ball, Princess Victoria," the girl in the grey dress said.

"Princess!" Olivia exclaimed. Victoria didn't look like any of the fairy-tale princesses in her books.

"Yes, and if she doesn't go to the ball we are both going to be in big trouble," the girl said. "I'm Beth, by the way."

"I'm Grace. That's Olivia and the kitten's name is Cuddle. Maybe we can help," Grace said. Beth looked relieved.

"That would be lovely, thank you." She lowered her voice so that Victoria couldn't hear. "Princess Victoria never wants to put on her pretty dresses and join in with the royal duties. I don't know why. The masked balls are such fun!"

Grace and Olivia shared a glance. Grace could guess what Olivia was thinking. Olivia felt sure she knew what Grace would say next.

"Cuddle's brought us here to help the princess!" both girls whispered at the same time.

Grace smiled her biggest smile.

"I'll get Princess Victoria back to her bedroom," she told Beth. She leapt up, pulling herself on to the lowest branch.

"Race you to the top of the tree!" Grace called to Victoria.

"You're on!" Victoria shouted back. Within moments, they had both disappeared among the branches.

"Come on, Cuddle!" Olivia called.

Cuddle scampered back down the tree and rubbed against the hem of Beth's dress.

"I'll show you to Princess Victoria's bedroom," the maid said as she started walking towards the palace's main entrance.

"If we work together, I bet we can get the princess to go to the ball," Olivia said.

"I hope so, or her parents will be disappointed," Beth said. "Princess Victoria is finally old enough to stay up for the masked ball and the king and queen are expecting to see her there."

Beth led Olivia and Cuddle up

the broad marble steps to the grand doorway. A footman bowed as they entered the palace.

Beth raced up a wide staircase in the hallway with Olivia and Cuddle right behind her.

They walked down a long corridor, passing marble statues and rows of oil paintings, and stopped in front of a large wooden door. Carved into the surface was the letter 'V'.

Beth looked left and right. "Let's be quiet. I could get into trouble if anyone sees you near the private quarters."

Beth pushed the door open and she, Olivia and Cuddle slipped in.

Princess Victoria's bedroom was like nothing Olivia had ever seen before. The thick carpet was a deep pink, and lilac curtains covered the windows. Victoria's dressing table had a pearl-edged mirror hanging over it and was stacked high with jewellery boxes. On the wall was a glass cabinet filled with glittering tiaras. But Olivia couldn't help noticing the muddy shoes and riding boots hiding beneath the princess's bed too!

The room had three wardrobes, each with frilly dresses spilling from them. In among all the dresses were a few pairs of canvas trousers, perfect for a tomboy to climb in.

"I win!" Victoria shouted from outside. The princess and Grace climbed through the window and landed with a thud on the floor. As they scrambled to their feet, Grace gave Olivia a wink. Victoria looked even dirtier than before.

"Now we can have our own party!" The princess grabbed Beth's hands and whirled her around the room. Victoria's face was bright with excitement, but Beth gently pulled her hands away.

"We can't." Beth sighed. "You need to go to the ball and greet your royal subjects."

"It'll be fun!" Olivia said.

Beth took Victoria's hand. "Just think how happy you'd make the king and queen."

But the princess sat down sadly on the bed. "Mummy and Daddy don't understand," she said, staring at the carpet. "They think it's fun, wearing crowns and frilly clothes, but it makes me feel so silly. I wish I could keep them happy, but I just don't want to go!"

Chapter Four
Feline Fashion Fix

"Miaaaaaooooow!" Cuddle fell out of one of the wardrobes, landing with a *flump* in a tangle of dresses. A silver bracelet nestled between her ears.

"Look, Victoria – Cuddle's a princess too!" Olivia said.

A small smile floated on Princess Victoria's lips. "Maybe she could go to the ball instead of me."

Grace hurried over to help Olivia tidy up and whispered in Olivia's ear. "I've got an idea for how we can get Victoria to go to the ball!"

Grace picked up a silver scarf and knotted it around her forehead. She grabbed an umbrella from one of the wardrobes and swiped it through the air like a sword.

"Ahoy there," she said in a growling voice. "I'm not Grace – I'm a pirate! I sail my ship on the seven seas, and if

you don't do what I say, I'll make you
walk the plank."

Princess Victoria giggled. "I love
to pretend!"

Beth tossed Victoria an umbrella
and Victoria and Grace ran around
the room, pretending to sword fight.

After a while, Grace lowered
her umbrella sword and smiled at
Victoria. "You could pretend that you
like dressing up and going to balls,"
she said, in her normal voice.

"It's easy – just imagine you're
acting on stage," Olivia added.

"That's a good idea," Beth said. "Go

on, Your Highness – just for tonight."

There was a sudden movement as Cuddle scrabbled around in the pile of dresses. She twitched her whiskers, and a pink dress floated across the carpet. It landed at Olivia's feet.

Princess Victoria gasped. "Cuddle's magic?"

"I think she's deciding what we should wear to the ball," Olivia said.

Cuddle's whiskers twitched again. A polka-dot dress moved towards

Grace. She held it up and showed the girls the deep pockets on each side.

"It's like my combat trousers back home."

Next, Cuddle pushed against Beth's ankles, nudging her towards a shimmering blue gown covered in sparkly sequins.

Beth's eyes shone as she picked it up.

Then the little kitten sat beside a white dress embroidered with tiny flowers. The sleeves were edged with red ribbons and it had an underskirt of red lace. Cuddle stared hard at Princess Victoria.

"Why don't you try it on?" Grace asked.

Princess Victoria picked up the dress. "It's all ... frilly. Do I really have to wear it?"

Cuddle threw back her head and yowled.

"Miaowwwooowwwooowww!"

"I think that's a yes," Olivia said, laughing.

But Victoria shook her head and dropped the dress on to the floor.

"Sorry, Cuddle. Dressing up just isn't any fun!"

Olivia's heart sank. How could they persuade this tomboy princess to go to the ball?

Chapter Five
Dressing-up Fun

Cuddle crept towards the princess's bare feet. She shook her head so her whiskers brushed over them.

"Hee hee!" giggled Victoria.

Grace turned to Olivia and Beth. "I think Cuddle's got a plan," she whispered excitedly.

The kitten swished her curly tail against Victoria's ankles.

"That tickles!" the princess squealed. Cuddle flicked her tail again and Victoria spun away from Cuddle, shaking with laughter.

"It's like you're dancing!" Grace cried, watching Princess Victoria skip and leap around the room to escape Cuddle's tickles.

The princess stopped in her tracks. "Dancing would be fun." Victoria glanced at the dress that Grace had grabbed from the floor.

Grace yanked down the zip and held it out, the opening of the dress gaping wide. "Just give it a try," she said. Cuddle mewed gently as if she was saying the same thing.

After a few moments, Princess Victoria gave a nod. "All right, then!"

Olivia and Beth helped the princess climb out of her canvas trousers whilst she hopped from foot to foot, laughing. Grace waited for Victoria to step into the dress, then – *zip!* – she fastened the back up.

"That was wonderful," the princess said. She knelt down and stroked Cuddle's silky head. "I didn't know dressing up could be so much fun."

"Does this mean you'll go to the ball?" Grace asked.

Princess Victoria frowned. But then a smile tugged at the corners of her mouth.

"Yes," she said. "I'll do it. I'll go to the ball. But only if you three come

with me – and you, Cuddle." Victoria
stroked Cuddle from the tip of her
nose to the black tip of her tail.

"Of course we will!" Olivia cried.

Princess Victoria grinned. "And
after the ball, we can have our own
party here."

"Hooray!" Grace and Olivia
cheered.

Olivia picked up the pink dress
and shrugged it over her head. Grace
and Victoria did up the tiny buttons

at the back, while Beth arranged the petticoats so they hung properly. Even Cuddle tugged the frilly edges with her teeth, pulling them straight.

Then Grace stepped into the polka-dot dress, and the other girls did up the hook-and-eye fastenings. Victoria picked up the blue sequinned dress.

"It's your turn, Beth," she said.

"I'm not sure –" Beth began.

But Olivia held the dress up against her, covering her maid's uniform. "You're going to look so pretty," she said.

"All right, then." Beth took off her uniform, folding it neatly and placing it on the bed. She stood quietly as

Grace and Victoria buttoned the dress up.

The four girls stood together in front of the pearl-edged mirror.

"Now for the final touch," said Princess Victoria. Rummaging in her wardrobe, she selected for each of the girls a pair of satin slippers that matched their dresses.

"We look like real princesses!"
Olivia said.

But a sob broke from Beth.

"I'm not a princess." A tear trickled
down her cheek. "I can't go to the ball.
If anyone recognizes me, I could get
into big trouble."

Grace and Olivia shared a doubtful glance.

Victoria folded her arms. "We can't go to the ball without Beth."

Chapter Six
Four Princesses

"Miaow!" went Cuddle, leaping on to the dressing table. She twitched her whiskers and a cloud of gold glitter descended over the girls. As it drifted to the floor they gazed at each other in astonishment. They were all wearing masks, magically given to them by Cuddle! Each was a different colour, to match the girls' dresses.

The eye slits were almond-shaped, and whiskers made from feathers were glued beside the ridge of the nose. On the top of each was a pair of pointed ears.

"Cat masks!" Olivia cried.

Grace took Beth's hand. "They're the perfect disguise," she said. "No one at the ball will know we're not all princesses."

"Please say you'll come," Princess Victoria begged.

Beth smiled. "I will! I'll be a princess for one night."

The four girls grabbed one anothers' hands, skipping round in a circle.

Knock knock knock.

The girls froze. Cuddle's ears flicked towards the door.

"Come in!" Princess Victoria called.

The door opened and an elderly man in a black suit and white gloves stepped inside.

"Are you ready, Your Highness?" he asked. His watery eyes widened as he saw the other girls, and he bowed.

"I beg your pardon. I didn't realize that other young ladies were present."

Princess Victoria winked at Beth.

"See?" she whispered. "Even Graves the butler doesn't recognize you." She spoke louder. "Graves, please may I introduce Princess Olivia, Princess

Grace . . . and Princess Elizabeth."

The butler gave a deep bow. "It's an honour to meet you," he said, straightening up. The girls could hardly stop smiling.

Cuddle jumped on to the floor and rubbed against Graves's polished shoes.

"Are you ready to go to the ball too, little one?" he asked.

"We're all ready, Graves," Princess Victoria replied. "Including Cuddle."

Graves coughed. "Forgive me, Your Highnesses, but aren't you forgetting something?"

"Of course," Victoria cried. "Tiaras!"

She opened the cabinet and passed a tiara to each of the girls. Each one was covered with clusters of tiny sparkling diamonds.

Graves helped the girls fit them behind the pointed ears of their cat masks.

"I feel like a real princess now," Olivia whispered to Grace.

The girls followed Graves back
along the corridor and down the
stairs, carefully holding up the hems
of their dresses so they wouldn't trip.
At last they arrived at the ballroom
door. Smoothing down their silk
skirts, Grace and Olivia peeked at
Princess Victoria and saw her face

blushing with nervous excitement.
Graves opened the door and they all
stepped inside, among the whirling
dancers.

"What do we do now?" Princess
Victoria asked.

"Enjoy ourselves!" Olivia cried.
She pointed to a group of boys and

girls gathered on the other side of the ballroom. "Let's go and say hello."

Grace tucked Cuddle into one of the deep pockets of her dress and the girls weaved through the crowd.

As they passed the band, a man in a bear mask shot his elbow out, knocking into Beth. The ribbons tying her mask in place fell loose, revealing part of her face.

"Oh, I'm so sorry, Your Highness!" the man cried.

"It's fine," Beth said. But her fingers trembled as she tried to refasten the ribbons.

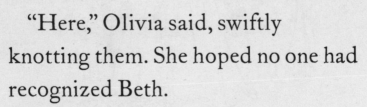

"Here," Olivia said, swiftly knotting them. She hoped no one had recognized Beth.

"Oh no," Beth muttered and ducked behind Olivia and Grace. The girls glanced up to see the king and queen heading their way. Olivia and Grace

fanned out their dresses and stood on
their tippy-toes trying to hide Beth,
but it was too late.

The king and queen walked right
up to them. Following Princess
Victoria's lead, the girls curtsied
politely. Beth tried to keep her head
down.

"Victoria," the king said when
he reached his daughter, "aren't
you going to introduce us to your
friends?"

Grace swallowed. Were they going
to be in trouble for bringing Beth to
the ball?

Chapter Seven
Trying Something New

"This is . . ." Princess Victoria started, her voice shaking, "Princess Olivia and Princess Grace, who have come to visit from a faraway land." She looped her arm through Beth's. "And this is . . ."

"Ah, yes of course, it's your friend Beth," the queen said.

"I am so sorry," Beth said in a shaky

whisper. She ducked in a quick curtsy.

"Sorry?" the queen repeated, glancing at her husband. "Why are you sorry? We're so glad to see you enjoying the ball."

The queen hitched up her velvet skirts so that she could kneel beside the girls. Her blue eyes were sparkling and a golden crown rested on her head, among her blonde curls.

She wore an emerald bracelet on her wrist and round her waist was a thick green silk sash.

"I'm so glad you've brought Victoria here," she whispered. She looked from Grace to Olivia, and back to Beth. "The three of you must be very special girls indeed."

The king helped his wife back to her feet, nodding in agreement. He was wearing a crown too – it looked very heavy on his head. His waistcoat was embroidered with gold thread and his jacket was made of gold satin.

"Enjoy yourselves!" he cried, flinging out an arm to take in the ball. "That's what tonight is all about."

Then the two of them disappeared into the crowd, nodding and smiling to people.

Cuddle wriggled out of Grace's pocket, darting through the legs of the dancers so that Princess Victoria skipped after her.

She scooped the little kitten up in her arms.

"Oh, Cuddle!" she gasped. "You're leading me on a dance again."

A crowd of boys and girls in animal masks gathered around her and Cuddle.

"I've always wanted to meet a real princess," a little girl in a butterfly mask said.

Princess Victoria's eyes flicked between Olivia and Grace, as if she didn't know how to reply. Grace cupped her hand and whispered in the princess's ear.

Victoria nodded at Grace, and then spoke to the girl. "And I've always wanted to meet a butterfly. What an amazing mask!" The girl gave a delighted squeal.

Princess Victoria chatted to all the

other children, turning to Grace and
Olivia when she wasn't sure what to
say. Olivia bobbed her head in time to
the music, making her curls bounce.
"Let's dance!" she cried. The four
girls held hands and twirled to the
music, their dresses billowing out so
they looked like spinning tops.

Cuddle scampered happily among
their feet.

"This way!" Olivia called, leading
the others in a gallop across the
ballroom, winding in and out of the
swirling crowd.

The song came to an end and the
girls collapsed on to a set of gilt
chairs, giggling and gasping for air.

Somewhere in the room, a trumpeter sounded a fanfare and Graves's voice boomed out.

"Their Royal Majesties would like to give a speech!"

The crowd of guests parted as the king and queen stepped through the room. Two footmen placed thrones beside the band and the king and queen swept towards them, waving to the crowd.

"Come on," Princess Victoria said, leaping up from her seat. She pulled the other girls to their feet and began to race through the crowd. The girls ran over to the raised platform, where the king and queen sat. The king cleared his throat and spoke loudly.

"It is my pleasure to present to you tonight, on the occasion of her first royal masked ball, my daughter, Princess Victoria." The king reached for his daughter's hand and she stepped up on to the stage next to her parents.

Everyone cheered as Princess Victoria waved to the crowd.

"Victoria, we're so proud of you for coming to the ball," the king whispered to his daughter. "We know you don't usually like this sort of thing."

"My friends showed me that it's nice to try something new," the princess said, smiling at the girls. Her eyes suddenly widened.

"But I'll still be allowed to climb trees, won't I?"

"Of course," the queen said. "We would never stop you from being who you are."

The king stroked his beard, looking at the grandfather clock that stood by the wall. "It's almost midnight," he said. "Time for bed." Princess Victoria grinned.

"Bedtime's the best time of all."

Chapter Eight
Sweet Dreams

The four girls sat cross-legged together on Victoria's bed. Victoria, Grace and Olivia had changed into their bedtime clothes.

"The ball wasn't so bad," Princess Victoria said, "but sleepovers with friends are more fun!"

Beth was still wearing her blue sequinned dress.

"I think I'm going to keep it on a bit longer," she said, stroking the skirts.

Beside Victoria's bed was a golden platter of fruit – juicy slices of pineapple, a pile of ruby cherries, oranges and tiny plates of raisins.

On a small card was a note in

beautiful writing. It read:

'To some very special girls,

Enjoy your feast (and don't stay up too

late!). Love, the king and queen.

Cuddle curled into a ball on a
silken pillow
as the girls dug
into their feast.

After they'd
eaten, Olivia
shook out her
black curls and Beth wove them into
a French plait.

Grace and Victoria pretended to be
sword fighters again but finally fell
on the bed laughing.

"I've had so much fu-u-u-un," Princess Victoria said, her words turning into a yawn. "Thank you for helping me today." She stretched her arms and lay down against the soft pillows.

Beth curled up beside her. "I'll never forget meeting you two and Cuddle," she murmured, her eyes drifting closed.

The room was quiet except for the soft sound of their breathing.

Grace and Olivia carefully climbed off the bed.

"I've had a wonderful time," Olivia whispered. She rubbed her eyes. "But I'm feeling sleepy too."

Cuddle jumped off the bed, landing beside their slippered feet. As she wound  through their legs, the girls felt the familiar tickling sensation.

"It's time to go home," Grace said.

***

When the girls opened their eyes again, they were back in Olivia's bedroom. Cuddle was perched on the chest of drawers, watching them.

Olivia smiled at Grace.

"Didn't I say you'd make a lovely princess?"

Grace laughed. "It was fun to do something different," she said. "Maybe tomorrow you could try wearing my combat trousers."

Olivia nodded. "I'll even add wellies and a rucksack," she said. "If Victoria can do it, so can I!"

Both girls gave loud yawns and snuggled down under the covers of Olivia's bed.

Cuddle jumped down on to the bed, touching her nose to Grace's and then Olivia's in a goodnight kiss.

"Goodnight, Cuddle!" both girls cried. "See you soon!"

The little kitten disappeared in a puff of sparkles, which shimmered over the girls like stars.

Olivia murmured drowsily, "Goodnight, Grace. Sweet dreams!"

Can't wait to find out
what Cuddle will do next?
Then read on! Here is the first chapter
from Cuddle's fourth adventure,
SCHOOL OF SPELLS . . .

School of Spells

Olivia squeezed her eyes shut. "Abracadabra, fiddle-de-dee, show me my wand, as fast as can be!"

She opened them again and looked at the dressing-up box on the lawn of her back garden. A pirate hat, face paints and a pink feather boa were spilling out of it, but Olivia sighed. "I can't see my wand anywhere," she said to Grace.

The two girls were in fancy dress. Olivia's fairy outfit was a purple leotard and tutu and pink net wings covered in silver sparkle. Her mum had made the outfit for Olivia on her sewing machine. Slung over her shoulder was the little bag she took everywhere.

Grace was dressed up as an elf, in green shorts and T-shirt, and pointy plastic ears hooked over her real ones.

"Don't worry," Grace said, "my mum says I'm good at finding things. When we lived on a farm, I used to look for where the chickens had laid their eggs. I'll help you find your wand."

It was a grey day in Catterton, with clouds squatting low over the houses and blocks of flats. Olivia and Grace had decided to brighten up the garden, turning it into a fairy grotto. Olivia had strung daisy chains from the branches of the trees, while Grace had lined up her mum's garden gnome collection on top of the fence.

The girls knelt beside the pot plants on the patio, searching among the leaves and flowers.

"If only I was a proper fairy," Olivia said. "Then I could use magic to find it."

Grace jumped up, her eyes shining.

"We do know someone with real magic."

"Cuddle!" Olivia cried. The girls grinned at each other. Cuddle was a cute kitten who took them on amazing magical adventures.

Just then, a beam of sunlight reached through the clouds. It shimmered in the air like a golden rainbow, shining right on to the dressing-up box.

Jingle jangle jingle jangle jingle.

"That's Cuddle's bell!" Grace cried. "She's here!"

The girls ran towards the dressing-up box and looked inside. Its contents wobbled, and a black-and-white tail with a kink in its tip poked through. Then came a pair of black paws, and finally a furry white face.

"Cuddle!" Olivia exclaimed. "And look what she's found."

The kitten had a purple plastic wand in her mouth. Olivia tucked it inside her bag.

"Clever Cuddle," Grace said, and tickled the kitten under the chin, just where her purr was rumbling.

With a miaow, Cuddle sprang into Grace's arms, the silver bell on her pink collar jangling. Both girls shut their eyes as the kitten's purr made their skin tingle all over.

"I feel like I'm covered in fizzy sherbet," Olivia murmured. "I wonder where Cuddle will take us this time . . ."

***

To find out what happens next,
get your copy of
School of Spells today!

Magical Friends

Meet Olivia, Grace and Cuddle in their first adventure!

New friends Olivia and Grace are amazed when cute kitten Cuddle appears and whisks them away to an ancient Egyptian pyramid. Can they help Beset find the Pharaoh's kitten inside it?

Find out in MAGICAL FRIENDS...

Superstar Dreams

Is Chloe brave enough
to perform on stage?

Cuddle uses her
magic to take
Olivia and Grace
backstage at a
talent show. Can
the girls persuade
talented Chloe
to audition even
though she's lost
her lucky charm?

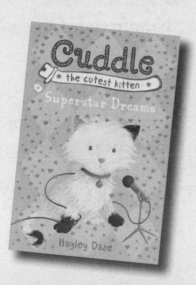

Find out in SUPERSTAR DREAMS...

Cuddle
★ the cutest kitten ★

School of Spells

Join Cuddle, Grace and Olivia
on a magical school adventure!

Cuddle takes the
girls to a school
with a difference
– the pupils are
enchanted creatures
and the lessons are
magical! But will
they be able to help
a shy unicorn make
some friends?

Find out in SCHOOL OF SPELLS...

Puddle
the naughtiest puppy

If you liked Cuddle the Cutest Kitten
you'll love Puddle the Naughtiest Puppy!

Puddle is a mischievous puppy who
appears every time it rains. He only has
to jump into a puddle to take cousins
Ruby and Harry on a series of amazing
magical adventures.

Why not begin your Puddle
collection today?

Getting to know your cat

Grace, Olivia and Cuddle have lots of fun on their adventures together, but real cats and kittens need a lot of looking after. That's why our friends at Cats Protection are going to be joining us in each book to talk about everything a cat needs for a happy home life.

Cats Protection want to make sure that every cat in their care finds a good home for life. This means talking to potential new owners about the kind of cat they are looking for, as every cat has its own individual personality. Once you get to know your own cat you should be able to work out how they are feeling quite quickly.

Always remember, Cuddle is a magical kitten, while real cats and kittens are living animals who need a lot of care, love and attention.

How do cats behave?

• A happy cat curls up when he sleeps, and his tail is relaxed. Sometimes you can hear him purr.

• A scared cat wants to escape and hide. His tail is low and tucked between his legs.

• A cat trusts you if he rubs his head or body against you and blinks slowly at you.

• An angry cat sticks his tail up in the air and may hiss at you. He may scratch or bite if he isn't left alone.

Congratulations – now you've learnt to tell how your cat is feeling. Next time we'll have some fascinating cat facts for you. See you then!

Cats Protection is the UK's leading feline welfare charity. Cats Protection has been helping cats since 1927 and each year they help more than 215,000 cats and kittens, giving them the chance of a better life.
To find out more please go to: www.cats.org.uk
For more cool cat facts, games and downloads, visit www.cats.org.uk/cats-for-kids

Pretty Princesses

Study the picture of the four girls below. Can you work out which one of the pictures opposite exactly matches this picture?

A

B

C

D

Answer at the back of the book

Mystery Circles

A part of a character is shown in each circle. Look at the clues and see if you can work out who is who!

1. I would love to be a princess.

2. I'm a maid who looks after Princess Victoria.

3. I am a princess, but I don't like dressing like one.

4. I serve the royal family.

Answers at the back of the book

Cuddle
★ the cutest kitten ★

To find out more about the adorable
Cuddle and her magical adventures, visit

www.ladybird.com/cuddlethekitten

Read hints and tips on how to look after
your own cat from Cats Protection,
plus download lots of fun activities.

Find more fantastic Ladybird titles at
www.ladybird.com

Answers to Cuddle Puzzles:
Pretty Princesses: Picture D is exactly the same.
Mystery Circles: 1: Olivia. 2: Beth. 3: Princess Victoria.
4: Graves.